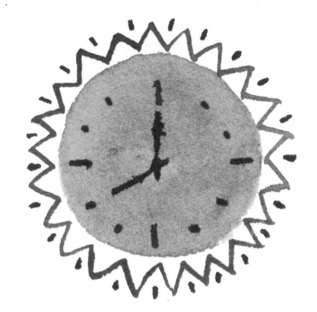

It's time for bed, Fred!

Oh no, Fred,
where are you going?

Fred?

That's not your bed, Fred!

Fred?
What are you doing
up there?

Trees are no places
for dogs.

UH-OH!

Where's your bed, Fred?

Watch out for the **muddy puddle**...

Too late!

Oh, Fred, you are **filthy.**

Bath time!

Wait, Fred, wait!

You're not dry yet.

Oh dear.

Come on, Fred.
It's time for bed.

Fred?

Fred?

Fred?

It's **very** late now, Fred.
Time for bed.

OK, you can have a story first.

But just one.

Now, where's your bed, Fred?

That's not your bed, Fred!

That's not your bed, Fred!

That's not YOUR bed, Fred!

Oh, Fred, that's MY bed!
Let's find your bed, Fred...

At last!

Night, night, Fred.
Sweet dreams!

For Alasdair

Bloomsbury Publishing, London, New Delhi, New York and Sydney

First published in Great Britain in 2013 by Bloomsbury Publishing Plc
50 Bedford Square, London, WC1B 3DP

Text and Illustration copyright © Yasmeen Ismail 2013
The moral right of the author/illustrator has been asserted

A CIP catalogue record for this book is available from the British Library

ISBN 978 1 4088 3700 9 (HB)
ISBN 978 1 4088 3701 6 (PB)
ISBN 978 1 4088 3946 1 (eBook)

1 3 5 7 9 10 8 6 4 2

C&C Offset Printing Co Ltd, Shenzhen, Guangdong

www.bloomsbury.com

Yasmeen Ismail

Time for Bed, Fred!

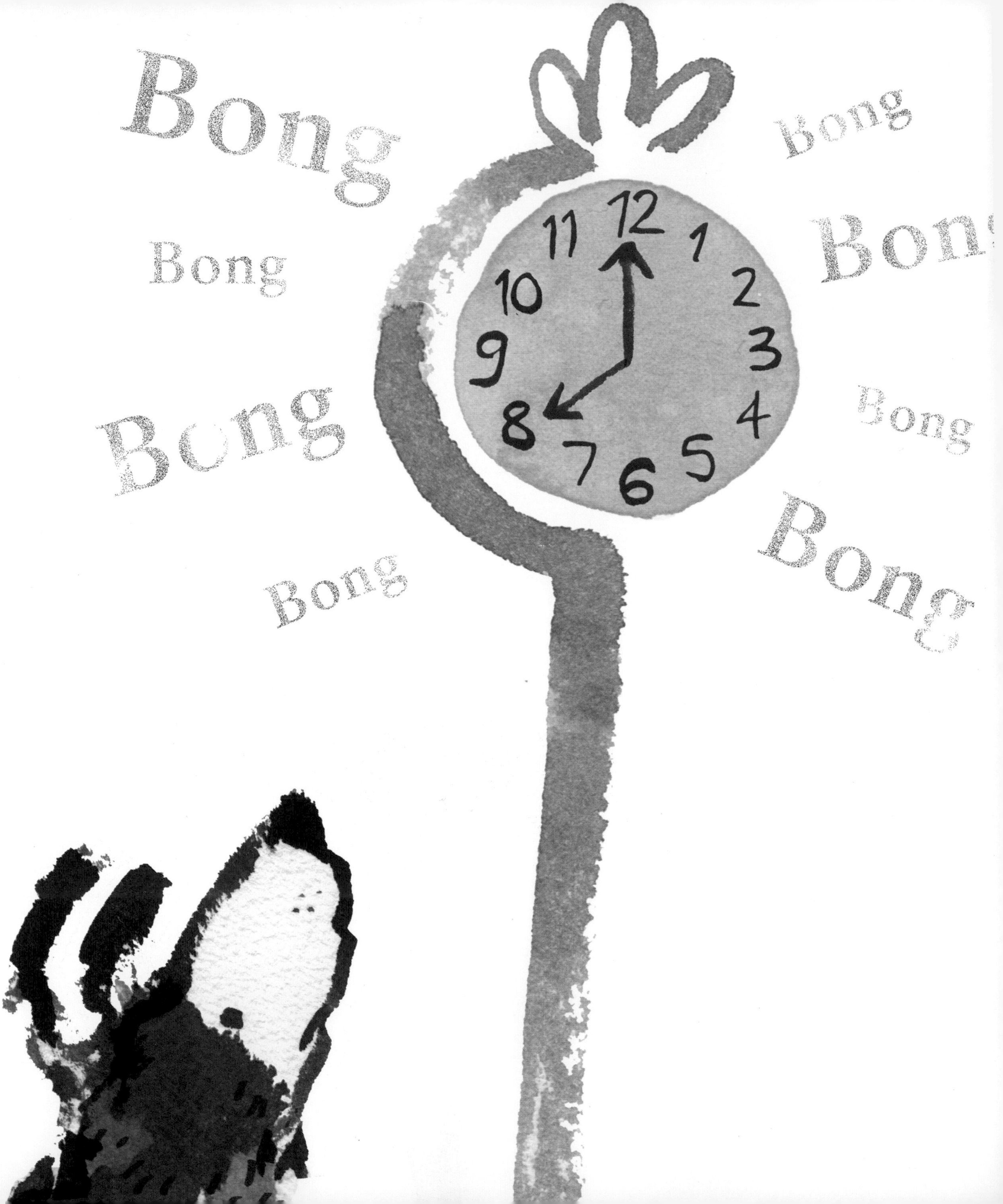
Bong
Bong
Bong
Bong
Bong
Bong
Bong
Bong
12
1
2
3
4
5
6
7
8
9
10
11